THE
Jolly Barnyard

BY ANNIE NORTH BEDFORD

ILLUSTRATED BY TIBOR GERGELY

GOLDEN PRESS • NEW YORK

Western Publishing Company, Inc., Racine, Wisconsin

T

Said Farmer Brown, "Tra-la, tra-lee!
Today is my birthday, lucky me!
I'll give my animals all a treat—
They'll get what they like best to eat."

He took a pan of oats, of course,
To the baby colt and the mother horse.

For the cow and the calf he set corn down,
"'Cause today is my birthday," said Farmer Brown.

The big white ram and the fat black sheep
Got lots of grain in a great big heap.

The gobbling turkey kept eating until
He had to admit he'd eaten his fill.

The chickens and rooster ate all their food;
There was more than enough for their hungry brood.

The duck ate her food, and so did the drake,
And so did their ducklings down by the lake.

The dog got bones to bury and chew.

The cat got milk, and her kitten did, too.

When all the animals had been fed,
Farmer Brown left, and the spotted cow said:

"Kind Farmer Brown! Wouldn't you say
We should give him a treat for his birthday?"

"Neigh! We'll pull his wagon without a jolt,"
Said the big brown horse and her little brown colt.

"Moo-oo!" said the cow. "I'll give him milk to drink."
Said her calf, "So will I, someday, I think!"

"Baa-aa! We'll give him fine wool," said the sheep,
"For our fleece is soft and warm and deep."

"Gobble!" said the turkey. "On Thanksgiving Day,
I'll dress up his table in my own special way."

"Cluck!" said the hen. "I'll give eggs fresh and white."
Said the rooster, "I'll wake him as soon as it's light."

"Quack!" said the duck and the drake. "Farmer Brown
Can make cozy pillows with our fluffy down."

"Bow-wow!" said the dog. "When the Farmer's away,
I'll watch over his house both night and day."

"Meow!" said the cat. "My brave kitten and I
Will catch all the mice—not a one will get by!"

Inside the farmhouse was one more fine treat—
A beautiful cake for the Farmer to eat.

Happy Birthday, Farmer Brown!